THE
HEARTSTOPPER
COLOURING BOOK

Also by
ALICE OSEMAN

HEARTSTOPPER
Volume One
Volume Two
Volume Three
Volume Four

Solitaire
Radio Silence
I Was Born for This
Loveless

THE

HEARTSTOPPER

COLOURING BOOK

ALICE OSEMAN

HODDER CHILDREN'S BOOKS

First published in 2020 by Hodder and Stoughton

7 9 10 8

This comic is drawn digitally using a Wacom Intuos Pro tablet directly into Photoshop CC.

A CIP catalogue record for this book
is available from the British Library.

ISBN 978 1 444 95877 5

Printed and bound in Great Britain by
Clays Ltd, Elcograf S.p.A

The paper and board used in this book
are made from wood from responsible sources.

Hodder Children's Books
An imprint of
Hachette Children's Group
Part of Hodder and Stoughton
Carmelite House
50 Victoria Embankment
London EC4Y 0DZ

An Hachette UK Company
www.hachette.co.uk

www.hachettechildrens.co.uk

www.aliceoseman.com

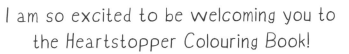

I am so excited to be welcoming you to
the Heartstopper Colouring Book!

When I started creating Heartstopper
as a webcomic in 2016, I dreamed that
I might be able to publish it in physical form
someday. And now it has its own
colouring book! I am endlessly grateful
to my readers for your support
over the years – it's thanks to your
enthusiasm that this book, and the rest
of them, exist in the first place.

These times are strange, but making art
has always brought me calmness when
the world feels a little chaotic.
I hope this book brings you that too.

So grab your pens and pencils,
find a place to snuggle up and chill,
and let's do some colouring!

Alice

x

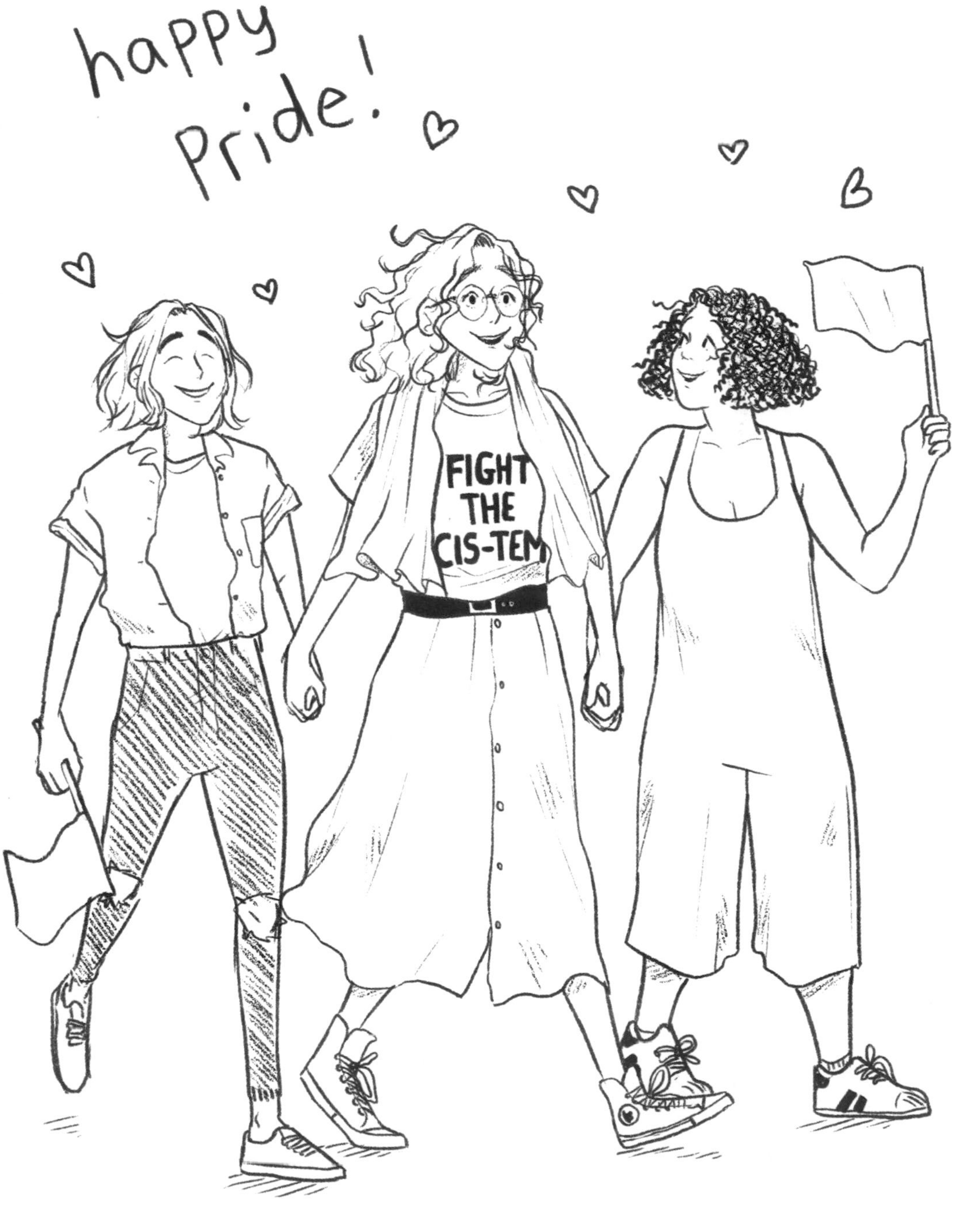
happy
Pride!
FIGHT
THE
CIS-TEM

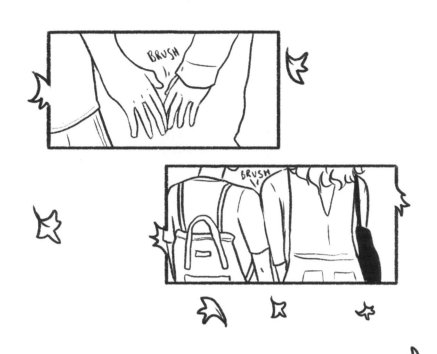

HAPPY
PRIDE!

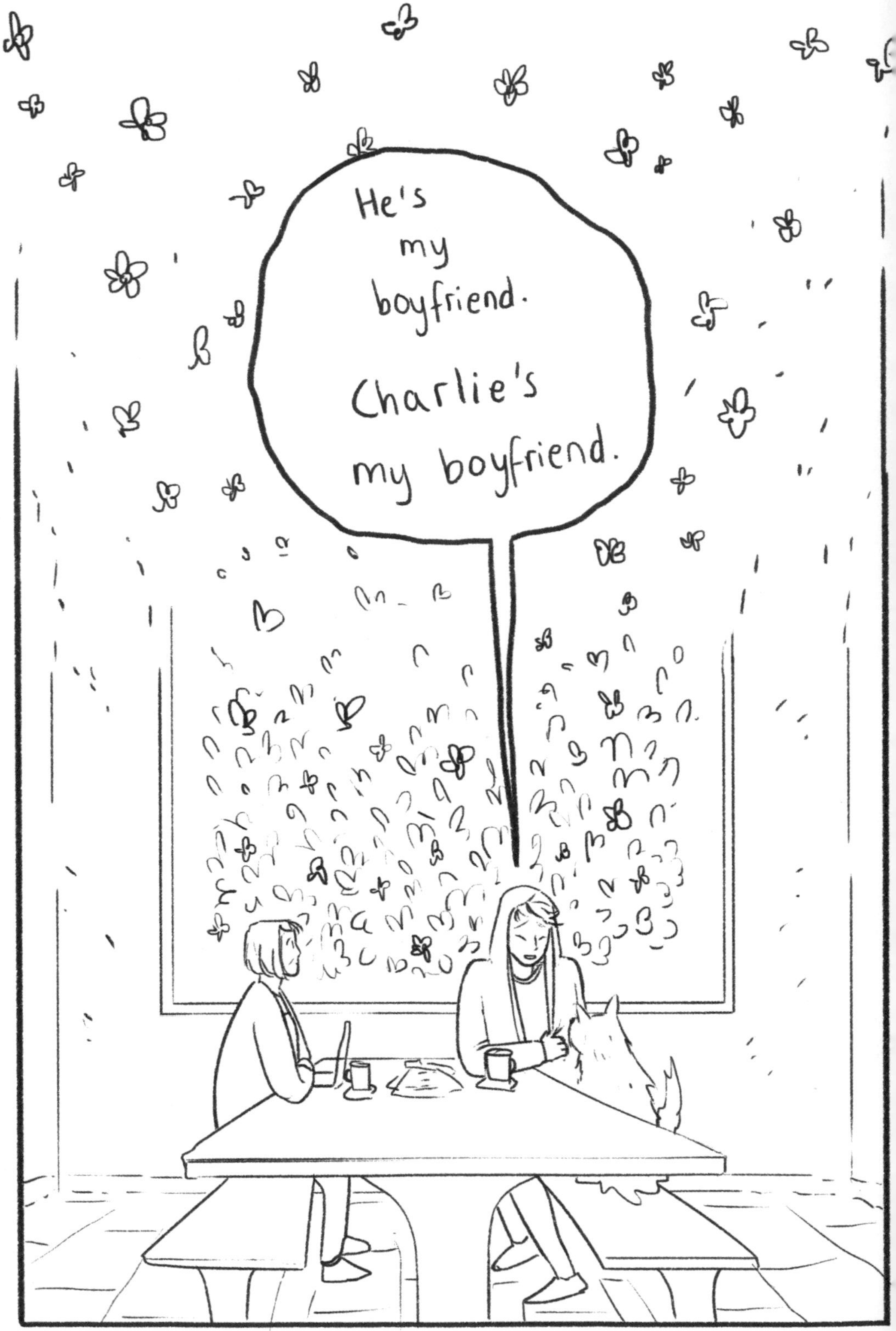
He's my boyfriend.
Charlie's my boyfriend.

Elle Argent

Nick's room

view A

view B

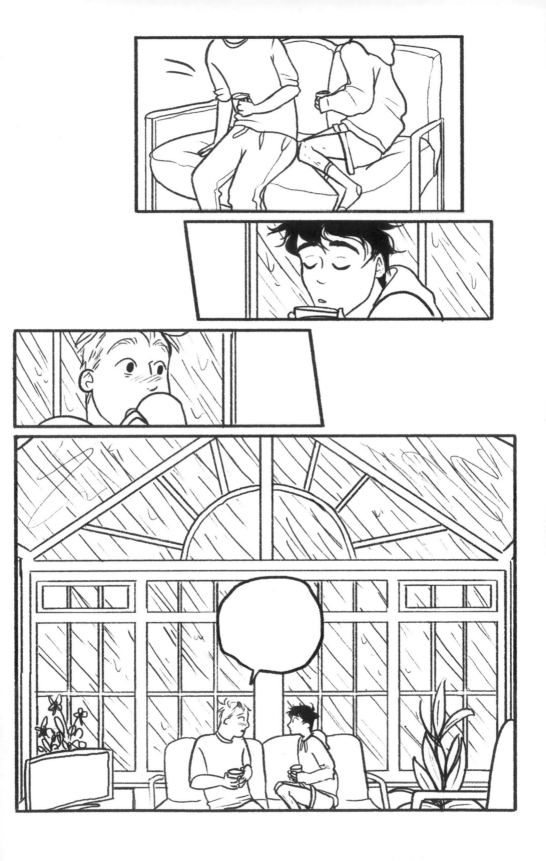

Charlie's room

View A

View B

happy pride!

SPLASH

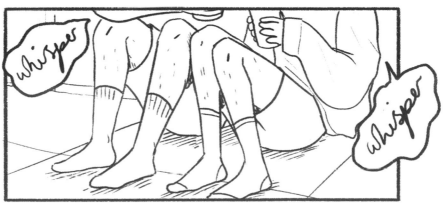

half an hour later...

PULL

Alice Oseman was born in 1994 in Kent, England, and is a full-time writer and illustrator. She can usually be found staring aimlessly at computer screens, questioning the meaninglessness of existence, or doing anything and everything to avoid getting an office job.

As well as writing and illustrating *Heartstopper*, Alice is the author of four YA novels: *Solitaire*, *Radio Silence*, *I Was Born for This* and *Loveless*, winner of the YA Book Prize.

To find out more about Alice's work, visit her online:

aliceoseman.com
twitter.com/AliceOseman
instagram.com/aliceoseman